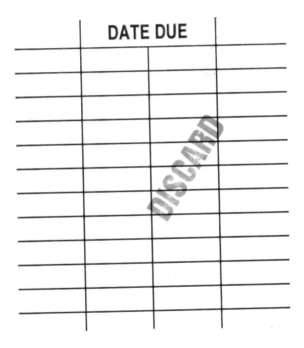

DATE DUE

The Kingdom

The Palace

Starless Forest

Burth

Mermaid's Cove

Crestwood

The Kingdom of Wrenly

2
The Scarlet Dragon

By Jordan Quinn
Illustrated by Robert McPhillips

LITTLE SIMON
New York   London   Toronto   Sydney   New Delhi

ABDOPUBLISHING.COM

Reinforced library bound edition published in 2016 by Spotlight, a division of ABDO, PO Box 398166, Minneapolis, Minnesota 55439. Spotlight produces high-quality reinforced library bound editions for schools and libraries. Published by agreement with Little Simon.

Printed in the United States of America, North Mankato, Minnesota.
092015
012016

THIS BOOK CONTAINS
RECYCLED MATERIALS

 LITTLE SIMON

An imprint of Simon & Schuster Children's Publishing Division
1230 Avenue of the Americas, New York, New York 10020

LIBRARY OF CONGRESS CATALOGING-IN-PUBLICATION DATA

This book was previously cataloged with the following information:

Quinn, Jordan.
 The scarlet dragon / by Jordan Quinn ; illustrated by Robert McPhillips. — First edition.
 pages cm. — (The kingdom of Wrenly ; 2)
Summary: A newly hatched, rare scarlet dragon comes under the special protection of the king and Prince Lucas, so when the dragon becomes ill, Lucas and Clara set out for the forest of Burth to find the vixberries needed for a cure.
ISBN 978-1-4424-9693-4 (pbk : alk. paper) — ISBN 978-1-4424-9694-1 (hc : alk. paper) — ISBN 978-1-4424-9695-8 (ebook)
[1. Adventure and adventurers—Fiction.
2. Dragons—Fiction. 3. Princes—Fiction. 4. Friendship—Fiction. 5. Kings, queens, rulers, etc.—Fiction.] I. McPhillips, Robert, illustrator. II. Title.
PZ7.Q31945Sc 2014
[Fic]—dc23
                    2013010841

978-1-61479-436-3 (reinforced library bound edition)

 **Spotlight**   A Division of ABDO | abdopublishing.com

CONTENTS

CHAPTER 1

Red Alert!

Plump juicy sausages, fresh fruits, warm cinnamon rolls, and fluffy scrambled eggs sat on the table in front of Prince Lucas. The prince drummed his fingers on the white tablecloth and stared dreamily at a tapestry of a unicorn and a lion. He had hoped to meet up with his best friend, Clara Gills. But breakfast had gotten in the way.

"You have to eat something before you go," said his mother, Queen Tasha.

Lucas grabbed an apple from the fruit bowl and took a big bite.

"There," he said in between chomps. *"Now* may I go?"

"Please don't talk with your mouth full," said his father, King Caleb.

"And you must wait to be excused," said the queen.

Lucas sighed and took another bite of his apple. He could hear a pair of boots clip-clopping along the

stone floor toward the great hall. Stefan, one of the king's men, entered the room and bowed his head. The king and queen looked up from their breakfast. Lucas stopped munching his apple.

"Your Highness," said Stefan, "I have some very strange news."

"What can it be?" asked the king.

"André and Grom have found an orphaned dragon's egg on the island of Crestwood," Stefan said.

André and Grom were wizardly brothers and the rulers of Hobsgrove, an island province of the kingdom of Wrenly.

"Well, that's not terribly unusual," said the king.

"True, my lord," said Stefan. "But this dragon egg is *red*!"

Everyone gasped—including the servants.

"My goodness!" exclaimed the king. "Are you sure?"

"Yes, I saw the egg myself, Your Majesty," Stefan said. "It's a deep scarlet red."

"Whoa!" Lucas cried. "That means it's a scarlet dragon!"

Lucas knew that a dragon was always the same color as its egg.

"That's impossible," the king bellowed. "According to the legends, there hasn't been a red dragon in the kingdom for more than two hundred years!"

The great hall became quiet. Nobody dared to challenge the king.

Then King Caleb stood up. "I must see this egg at once," he said.

"Yes, Your Majesty," said Stefan. "I'll summon the royal ship."

"Father, may I go with you?" asked Lucas.

The king raised an eyebrow.

"Please?" Lucas begged.

"I'd like to go too," the queen chimed in.

Then the king laughed. "Okay, we shall *all* go," he said. "We'll leave for the dock in a few minutes."

"Yes!" Lucas shouted as he jumped up from the table. Then he quickly sat back down. "May I please be excused?" he asked.

"You may," said his parents.

Lucas bolted from his seat and raced all the way to the stables.

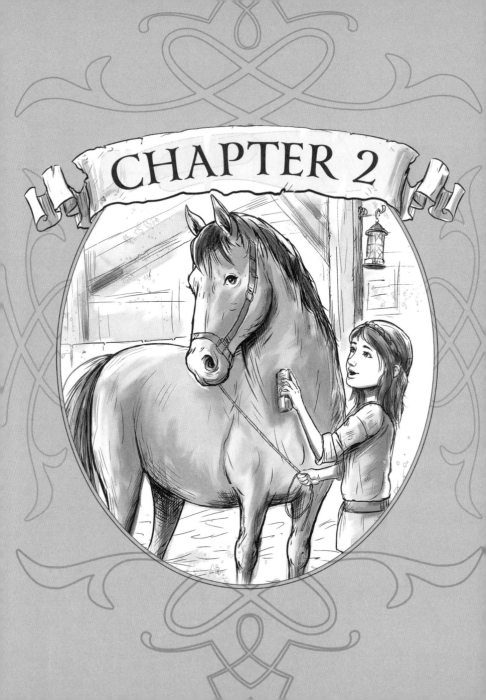

CHAPTER 2

A Fire Breather

Lucas spotted Clara outside a stall. He watched her gently brush her horse, Scallop. Scallop was a velvet-brown Arabian horse with a black mane, a black tail, and white socks. The horse had been a reward from King Caleb for finding Queen Tasha's lost emerald.

"Clara!" called Lucas. "You'll never guess what!"

Clara stopped brushing. Her green eyes lit up when she saw her friend.

"What?" she asked.

"André and Grom found a red dragon's egg on Crestwood!" said Lucas.

"A red dragon's egg!" exclaimed Clara. "Do you know what that means?"

"It means there's a scarlet dragon inside!"

"Exactly," said Clara. Then her face became serious. "And you know what they say about red dragons."

"Sure," answered Lucas. "The legends say they're the most magnificent dragons in all the world!"

"And the most feared," Clara added.

"Not to worry," Lucas said. "It's all in the training."

Clara rolled her eyes.

"Have you ever trained a fire-breathing dragon?" she asked.

"Actually, I've never even trained

a dog," Lucas said. "But the knights and wizards know all about dragon training."

"I suppose," said Clara. "But what if it sets Wrenly on fire?"

"Then we'll put the fire out," said Lucas. "Trust me. A red dragon is going to be amazing."

"Well, it certainly is exciting," Clara admitted.

Lucas gave Clara a pat on the shoulder.

"Well, I'd better be off," he said. "My parents are taking me to see the egg right now."

Clara waved as Lucas ran back to the castle.

CHAPTER 3

Eggshells

Lucas boarded the royal ship with his parents. It was a beautiful spring morning. The clouds had a reddish glow. *Maybe it's because there really WILL be a scarlet dragon in the kingdom of Wrenly,* he thought. Lucas grabbed the railing and looked toward Crestwood. He wished the ship would sail faster.

André met them at the dock.

"Come with me, Your Majesties," he said.

André showed the royal family to a waiting carriage.

"Where is the egg?" asked the king.

"Grom found it beside the lava flow."

"Are you sure the egg has been abandoned?" the king asked. He knew that mother dragons were very protective of their eggs.

"Yes," André said. "We've watched the egg for several hours, and there's been no sign of a mother."

"Why would the mother abandon her egg, anyway?" Lucas asked.

"Well, perhaps she feared the responsibility of raising a red dragon," André said. "One thing's for sure, she knew to keep the egg very warm."

"But I thought *all* eggs had to be kept warm," said Lucas.

"A scarlet dragon's egg must be kept near or over an open flame," André said. "I think she left the egg beside the lava on purpose."

"But these things are all based on legends," said the king. "Do you really believe in these stories?"

André looked thoughtful for a moment. "Well, we shall soon find out," he said.

The carriage bumped along the road. Soon they came to a clearing. Lucas could see the slow-moving lava. It oozed down the side of the volcano and into a creek that flowed into the sea. Steam rose from the creek where the lava met the water.

André parked the carriage and helped the king and

queen to the ground. Lucas jumped
to the dirt by himself.

"Over here!" shouted Grom as he
waved to the royal family.

André led the way to the dragon's egg. It sat nestled in a shallow hole next to the stream of lava. It was a deep scarlet red—just as Stefan had described.

The king kneeled beside the it. "It can't be . . . ," he whispered.

King Caleb began to inspect the egg. It was the size of a grapefruit. He looked at it from every angle. Then, with both hands, he gently lifted the egg to the light. Everyone could see the faint outline of the creature within. The king held the

egg to his ear and listened. Then he carefully placed it back into the hole. He looked at the two wizards and his family.

"I never would've thought it possible," said the king. "But this is indeed a scarlet dragon egg."

The queen clasped her hands together. "What an exciting thing to happen in the kingdom of Wrenly!" she exclaimed.

"I knew it!" declared Lucas. Then he grabbed his father's arm. "Can we take the dragon egg back to the palace?"

"No," the king said firmly. "The egg must remain in Crestwood until it hatches. It cannot be disturbed."

Lucas hung his head.

"But after the egg hatches," the king went on, "you may bring the baby dragon back to the palace."

"Will the baby dragon be mine?" asked Lucas.

"Yes," said the king. "I hereby proclaim the red dragon will be yours."

Lucas jumped into his father's arms and hugged him. "Thank you, Father! Thank you!"

"You are welcome, my son," the king said with a smile. "You must

take good care of your dragon. And with some help, you will learn to train him."

Then, with Lucas still attached, the king turned to Grom. "Will you continue to care for the egg until it hatches?"

Grom, who had raised many an orphaned dragon, knew exactly how to care for the egg.

"I would be honored, King Caleb," said Grom. "But I should like one thing in return."

The king raised an eyebrow. He

wasn't used to bargaining. No one would dare—except Grom. Grom was a slightly crafty wizard. He shared his great healing powers with the kingdom, but he could also be a troublemaker.

"And what would you like in return?" asked the king.

"I would like the scarlet eggshells after the dragon hatches," Grom said. Dragon eggshells were known to have magical powers. Grom was planning to use them in his potions.

"Very well," said the king. "I see no harm in it. You may have the shells."

Grom smiled crookedly. "Thank you, Your Majesty," he said.

CHAPTER 4

Nesting

News of the scarlet egg swept across the kingdom like dragon fire.

"It's a miracle!" some said. "A red dragon will surely bring good luck to the kingdom."

Others said, "Oh no! Scarlet dragons are bad luck. Nothing good can come from this."

The local merchants cashed in

on the news. An inn known as the Red Rooster had now become the Red Dragon. The grocer began to dye his eggs red. The village boys sold hand-carved red dragons by the side of the road.

But Prince Lucas had bigger things to think about. He had to design a lair for the scarlet dragon. Lucas and Clara learned everything they could about dragon lairs. They read books and talked to the knights and the wizards.

Then Lucas drew a plan for the
dragon's home. The main entrance,
which was behind the castle, looked
like the opening to a cave. Rocks and
boulders surrounded the mouth of
the cave. Lucas added a ledge for
the dragon to perch
on. Underground
tunnels formed

the inside. Each tunnel led to a chamber. Lucas drew a sleeping area, a dining space, and a playroom with a wading pool and a waterfall. He added a large fireplace to each chamber, because he read that red dragons needed their homes to be hot. Lastly,

he added an escape exit in case an enemy approached the lair.

Then Lucas presented his plan to his father. The king loved Lucas's ideas. He had his men draw up the official plan.

Meanwhile, Clara and Lucas planned to make chew toys for the baby dragon.

"I'll sew some stuffed animals," said Clara.

"I'll carve some wooden toys," Lucas said.

Over several weeks, Clara sewed and stuffed a rabbit, a bear, and a fox with her mother's fabric scraps.

Lucas collected branches from the woods and carved a sea serpent, a boot, a war hammer, and some bones. When they were done, they

stored the chew toys in a chest in Lucas's playroom until the lair was finished.

The king's men worked on the lair for two months. While they were building, Lucas took dragon training classes on Hobsgrove. André and Grom taught him how to feed and care for hatchlings. They also taught him about dragon discipline. Lucas shared everything he learned with Clara. He wanted his best friend to

help him raise the dragon.

Then one afternoon a trumpet sounded. The king's men announced that the lair had been completed! It was time for the royal family and Clara to have the grand tour. The children brought the dragon's toys.

Everyone followed Stefan into the lair. Torches lit the tunnels. Even though it was a warm summer day, fires crackled in each of the chambers. This is the temperature it would have to be for the baby dragon. The king and queen walked around excitedly. They were very impressed.

"A job well done," said the king.

"A splendid dwelling," said the queen.

"Now all we need is the baby dragon!" exclaimed Lucas.

When they got to the playroom,

Lucas and Clara laid out the chew toys. While Stefan talked to the king and queen, the children dipped their feet in the wading pool. They left the lair through the escape exit, which led them to the west side of the castle, under the bridge.

CHAPTER 5

The Hatchling

Stefan raced into the great hall.

"Hear ye! Hear ye! The time has come!" he shouted. "The dragon egg has begun to hatch!"

The royal family dropped everything they were doing and set sail for Crestwood. Again, André brought them to the dragon's egg. Sure enough, the egg had a crack that zigzagged across the middle.

"It won't be long," Grom said.

Everyone sat and waited. The egg lay very still. A hawk cried overhead. Quails rustled in the underbrush nearby. Wrens warbled in the treetops. Nobody said a word until the egg began to rock. It then wobbled and trembled. The egg rolled around, and then, all at once, the shell broke apart. And there in the center stood a very unsteady, very red baby dragon.

"*Aaack! Aaack!*" it cried, sticking out its red tongue.

The baby dragon was the size of

a kitten. It had the face of a lizard and horns on top of its head. It also had a long pointy tail, batlike wings, and two eyes that glowed like emeralds. The dragon was a stunning shade of crimson fire.

"It's extraordinary!" said André.

"It's adorable!" cried the queen.

"It's magnificent!" said Lucas.

"It's unbelievable!" said the king.

"It's a *boy*!" cried Grom, who swiftly swept the broken eggshells into a leather sack.

André lifted the dragon and let him perch on his arm. The hatchling steadied himself with his wings. André offered the dragon some spinach and berries. But the dragon didn't seem interested. He just wanted to perch.

"May I hold him?" Lucas asked.

André let the dragon step onto Lucas's outstretched arm. The dragon perched steadily.

"Lucas, you must take him to his lair right away," said André. "Food, home, and love are what the hatchling needs most now."

"Aaack! Aaack!" screeched the dragon.

Lucas gently pet the dragon's nubby horns. "Wow," he whispered. "My very own dragon."

CHAPTER 6

Redhead

Clara couldn't take her eyes off the baby dragon.

"He's beautiful," she said.

Even though they were in the lair, the dragon stayed on Lucas's arm.

"He thinks I'm his mother," said Lucas.

Clara laughed. "That's a good thing," she said. "Because you *are* his mother."

Lucas smiled. "Let's take him to the playroom and think of some names for him."

"I love to think up names!" Clara said.

They hurried down the tunnel to the lair's playroom. Lucas set the baby dragon on the floor. Then they

watched to see what he would do. The little dragon held out his wings and took a few quick steps.

"He is *so* sweet," Clara gushed. "Maybe we should call him Sweetie Pie."

"No way," said Lucas. "He needs a noble name."

They watched the baby dragon
chase his tail. He went round and
round. Then he noticed the chew
toys and pounced on the rabbit.
He batted it with his nose. Then
he brought it to Lucas
and dropped it on
the floor.

"Good boy,"
Lucas said.

Clara smiled.

Then the dragon lay down in front of Lucas.

"Awwww," he said. "The little guy needs a rest."

Lucas pet the dragon's horns.

"Let's think up more names," Clara said.

"Okay," said Lucas. "How about Firefly?"

"I like it," said Clara. "What about Fireball?"

"That's a good one," Lucas said.

They thought of all kinds of names: Mr. Flame, Big Red, Bonfire, and Rusty.

"What do you think of Ruskin?" asked Lucas.

"I really like it," said Clara.

"It means 'redhead,'" Lucas said.

"Even better!" said Clara.

"Okay! Then his name shall be Ruskin!" Lucas declared.

Then he addressed the baby dragon. "Hello, Master Ruskin," he said.

The dragon didn't respond.

"That's okay," Clara said. "He doesn't know his name yet."

Lucas tried again—a little bit louder this time. "Hey, Ruskin!"

Ruskin didn't react at all.

"Maybe he's hungry," Clara said.

Lucas offered the dragon some olives and rhubarb. Ruskin didn't even sniff the food.

"Maybe he's thirsty," said Clara. They carried Ruskin to the

wading pool. He just lay in a heap beside the water and didn't move.

"Uh-oh," said Lucas. "Something's wrong."

"You're right," said Clara. "He doesn't look well."

"We'd better get help," said Lucas.

"You go," said Clara. "I'll stay here."

Lucas ran as fast as he could to the castle.

CHAPTER 7

Vixberries

The king summoned André and Grom to help the sick dragon. The wizards brought herbs, magic stones, and charms to the lair. They mixed garlic, red nettle, and raspberry tea. Grom laid a circle of magic stones around the dragon. Then Grom opened Ruskin's mouth while André spoon-fed the potion. They rubbed ointment on the dragon's scales and

waved charms around his head. The wizards even gave him an herb bath. But Ruskin was still limp, and his eyelids drooped.

André stood before Lucas and the king.

"I'm afraid the hatchling is very

ill," he said. "I've seen this before. The illness comes on fast and rarely ends well."

"André, you have to help him," Lucas pleaded. "I don't want to lose him!"

"Nor do I," said the king.

André looked grim. "There's only one known cure," he said.

"What is it?" they asked.

"A combination of mint tea and vixberries," André said. "The trouble

is, vixberries were once plentiful in the kingdom. But now they're almost impossible to find."

"Nothing's too hard for the king's men," said the king. "I'll order a search party. Where shall I send them?"

"The Starless Forest on the island of Burth," said André. "The place where vixberries grow is said to be

enchanted. It's been a secret for generations, and no one knows just where they are."

"My men will scour the forest," said the king. "I will reward whoever finds the vixberries with twenty pieces of gold."

"If Ruskin is to live, we'll need the berries by sundown," said André.

"But that gives us only one afternoon!" cried Lucas.

"That's not enough time!"

Lucas's eyes filled with tears. King Caleb wrapped his arms

around his son and held him close.

"We have to have hope," said the king. Then he took off to organize the search party.

Clara put her hands on Lucas's shoulders.

"It'll be okay, Lucas," she said. "I have an idea."

Lucas wiped his eyes with the backs of his hands. "You do?" he said.

"Yes," she whispered. "But we have to leave at once."

Bren

Clara grabbed Lucas by the hand, and the two of them ran to the stables. After saddling Scallop and Lucas's horse, Ivan, they hopped on and galloped over the bridge to Burth.

"Where are we going?" shouted Lucas.

"You'll see!"

Clara and Lucas thundered along

a dirt road until they came to a stone cottage surrounded by orange lilies. Clara and Lucas tied Scallop and Ivan to a hitching post. Then Clara pounded on the door.

A short, stocky troll with rosy cheeks and sparkling blue eyes answered the door.

"Well, hello, Clara!" the young troll exclaimed. "Why the heavy hand? Are you delivering bread with your father today?"

Clara shook her head. "No, Bren," she said. "The prince and I have come to ask for your help. The scarlet dragon is very sick. He needs vixberries before sundown or he'll die."

The troll's expression became very serious.

"What makes you think I know anything about vixberries?" asked Bren.

"Because you told me about them one time, and nobody knows the Starless Forest better than you," said Clara. "Can you help us?"

Clara had known Bren ever since she could remember. They were the same age and often played together when her father delivered bread to his customers on Burth. Bren had shared magical stories about the Starless Forest.

Bren sighed as he thought about what Clara had just asked.

"The king has promised a generous reward," said Clara.

"Oh?" questioned Bren. "What kind of reward?"

"Twenty pieces of gold," Lucas replied. He knew that all trolls loved gold.

Bren looked around to see if anyone else was listening.

"Okay," said Bren. "I will get you vixberries."

Lucas and Clara clapped their hands.

"May we go with you?" asked Clara.

"No," Bren said. "The location is a secret. I'm the only one who knows. My father told me about it before he passed away."

"*Please?*" begged Clara.

"No way," said Bren.

"What if something happens to you?" asked Lucas.

"Then no one will ever know where the vixberries are," added Clara.

Bren knew this was true. He also knew he was going to have to tell

someone about the vixberries some-
day. He was almost certain Clara
and Lucas could be trusted.

"Perhaps you are right," he said.
"But you must promise never to tell
a soul."

"We promise," said Lucas and
Clara.

"Okay," said Bren. "Then we must leave right away if we hope to find the vixberries before sundown."

Bren gathered torches, water, and some leather pouches. He slung a wool bag with a long strap across his chest. Then he placed a worn felt hat on top of his head.

"Let's go," he said.

CHAPTER 9

The Breach

The children hiked through a field of cornstalks, which grew from the land that the trolls had farmed for hundreds of years. Lucas and Clara carefully followed Bren over a swaying rope bridge and into the Starless Forest. As they tramped along, Lucas told Bren about the baby dragon. The woods grew darker and darker. Soon it became too dark to see. Bren

lit a torch for each of them.
After a while he stopped
and put a hand to his ear. "Do
you hear that?" he asked.

Lucas and Clara stood still
and listened.

"It sounds like rushing water," Clara said.

"It's the Lost River," said Bren. "Follow me."

Lucas and Clara stayed close to Bren. Soon he stopped again, this time beside two enormous boulders. Bren reached into his wool bag and grabbed a handful of dried lavender petals. He sprinkled them over the boulders. The boulders began to rumble. Then an opening appeared.

Clara and Lucas gasped.

"What's going on?" Clara asked.

"This is the Breach," said Bren.

"What's that?" asked Lucas.

"It's an opening in the forest," said Bren. "It's the only place in the Starless Forest where the sun shines."

"But why?" asked Lucas.

"Long ago, a wizard enchanted

the place to protect the unicorns from being hunted."

"You mean unicorns really exist?" Lucas asked.

"Yes," said Bren. "But today only in the Breach."

"Wow," said Clara. "No wonder it's a secret."

"And a very sacred one," Bren said. "It's now the only place where the vixberries grow too. Follow me."

They climbed through the opening in the rocks. A tunnel twisted

and turned before them. As they walked, the sound of the water grew louder. Then they turned a corner, and suddenly the tunnel was filled with sunlight.

Lucas and Clara shaded their eyes with their hands. From the cave opening they could see a waterfall tumbling into a pool of sparkling water. A mother unicorn and her colt drank at the water's edge. Wrens twittered. The ground was covered with forget-me-nots: tiny sky-blue flowers with a white inner ring and a yellow center. Butterflies

flitted above the flowers.

"Wow. This is paradise," Lucas whispered.

"It's magical," said Clara.

"Come on," Bren said. "We'd better hurry."

They snuffed the torches and left them in the cave. Then they walked over to the water.

"Over there," Bren said.

He pointed to some thorny vines that had climbed the rocks beside the stream. Plump white berries dotted the vines.

"Those are vixberries," said Bren.

He handed a pouch to Lucas and one to Clara.

The kids scrambled toward the

vines and plucked the white berries.

Plop! Plop! Plop! They filled their leather pouches. When they were done, they lit their torches and retraced their steps through the tunnel and out of the forest. By the time the kids got back to Bren's cottage, the sun had already begun to go down.

"You must go," said Bren.

Lucas and Clara thanked their friend and promised not to say a word about the Breach.

"You'll get your reward," Lucas said.

Bren nodded. "Hurry," he said. "I hope it's not too late."

Lucas and Clara hopped back onto their horses and raced over the bridge and up the hill to the lair.

CHAPTER 10

Wake Up!

"Is Ruskin alive?" shouted Lucas as he entered the lair.

"Shhhh—don't startle him," said André, stroking Ruskin's head. "He's alive, but he's very, very sick."

"Here," said Lucas, handing André the pouches. "Clara and I brought you something."

"What's this?" asked André as he loosened the strings on one

of the pouches and peeked inside.
"Vixberries!" he exclaimed.

There was no time for questions. The wizards went right to
work. André poured the berries into

a mortar and crushed them with a pestle. Grom brewed some mint tea. As soon as it boiled, he poured it over the crushed berries. Then André stirred the mixture until it was blended. Grom opened Ruskin's mouth, and André fed the dragon a spoonful of the potion.

"Now what?" asked Clara.

"Now we wait," said André.

They sat and watched the baby

dragon. Ruskin just lay there. Grom checked Ruskin's pulse.

"Is he still alive?" asked Lucas.

"He's fallen asleep," said Grom.

"Perhaps you and Clara should

get some rest too," André suggested.

"No way," said Lucas. "I'm staying right here until he wakes up."

"Me too!" said Clara.

"Very well," said André.

Then André went to the palace. He told the king to call off the search party and gave him the latest news. When André returned, he brought  a loaf of bread and a large pot of wild rice soup with some bowls. Stefan followed with pillows and blankets.

"King Caleb will

allow you to stay," André said to the children.

They all ate supper as they watched over Ruskin. Grom set a plate of food in front of the dragon. Every few minutes Lucas checked to see if Ruskin was still breathing. Then, sometime before dawn, everyone fell fast asleep.

And that's exactly when Ruskin
woke up.

"*Aaack! Aaack!*" he squawked.

Lucas opened his eyes to find the
baby dragon sitting by his side and
looking into his eyes. The plate of
food beside Ruskin was empty.

"Ruskin!" he cried. "You're all better!"

Ruskin squawked again.

And it was true; Ruskin was well.

The next day the king and queen threw a dragon baby shower for the whole kingdom. Bren got his reward, and Lucas and Clara honored their promise to keep the Breach a secret.

And from that day forward, Ruskin began to grow. He also learned how to fly! Now the only thing Ruskin needed was training. Lots of training.

But that's another story.

The Kingdom of Wrenly

COLLECT THEM ALL!

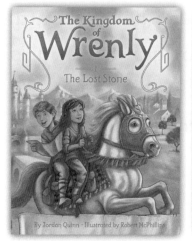

**Hardcover Book ISBN
978-1-61479-435-6**

**Hardcover Book ISBN
978-1-61479-436-3**

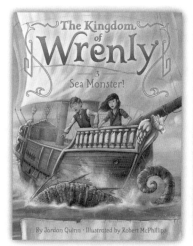

**Hardcover Book ISBN
978-1-61479-437-0**

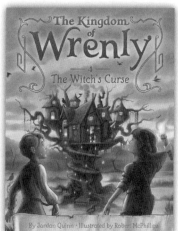

**Hardcover Book ISBN
978-1-61479-438-7**